Hi, my name is Hayden.

I'm nir of writ Califor

mine the past couple of years to write and illustrate a book about some of my current interests in science, sea animals, amphibians, reptiles, endangered animals, Minecraft, and more! I read many books on these subjects, watch videos, play Minecraft in creative mode, sketch, and draw in 3D and with the computer.

When I heard that Minecraft was going to add an axolotl to the game, a special type of salamander, I immediately started having a lot of ideas about the adventures the axolotl could go on. These ideas quickly turned into stories that I began putting onto these pages. I hope you enjoy reading the axolotl's big adventures!

I'd also like to say, "Thank you." Thank you to my parents, Nana, Rhonda Asbenson and wonderful teachers throughout the years who continue to guide me in realizing my dreams and expressing my ideas through writing and art.

The Axolotl: Adventures In Minecraft
Written and Illustrated by Hayden Coles

This book follows the Mojang commercial usage guidelines:

- This book is not an official Minecraft product and is not approved by or associated with Mojang.
- Mojang has no liability for this product or purchase.
- This product's seller and manufacturer/publisher is not Mojang, not associated with, or supported by Mojang.
- All rights (including copyright, trademark rights, and related rights) in the Minecraft name, brand, assets, and any derivatives are and will remain owned by Mojang.

Published by Dougy Press
dougypress.com

ISBN: 978-0-9797132-4-8

Contents

4

CHAPTER 1

LUSH CAVES

I f you follow azalea trees' roots, you'll eventually stumble into the openings of lush caves with freshwater ponds. In one of these lush caves lives a small, pink, axolotl. The axolotl loves his home there, but he's lonely. The only other types of life in the caves are many interesting plant varieties. Glow berry vines, spore blossoms, occasional drip leaf plants, azalea bushes, and moss are all growing in the axolotl's habitat.

The axolotl's cave provides him with glow berries to eat. The glow berries are shining bright yellow and are easy to find because they illuminate the cave. Jumping on drip leaf plants helps him reach the berries while staying moist. After a long day of catching glow berries, he lies down on the cozy moss on the bottom of the pond where he sleeps. When he wakes up, he explores more of his pond.

One day he finds a small secret passageway covered by foliage. He swims through the water to get to the passageway that's hidden by glow berry vines and normal vines.

"I really like this passageway, but where does it lead?" wonders the axolotl.

"It looks like it leads out to the blue waters of an ocean where I might find some friends to play with. Maybe I won't be lonely anymore with new friends!"

CHAPTER 2

LOST AT SEA

The axolotl swims slowly through the dark, watery passageway. At the end of the tunnel, he sees a vast ocean. Suddenly, a large wave sweeps him into the deep water, and he's pushed out to sea. "Oh, no! I need to get back home!" he yells. He uses all of his strength to swim back to the tunnel, but he does not have enough strength and energy to get home. As the day turns to night, he finds a coral reef, swims into a fire coral, and searches through the tubes. He finally finds a vast and hollow opening big enough for him to sleep in.

Overnight, the ocean currents sweep him out of the coral branch and onto the surface of the ocean where he drifts into a steel-gray bucket with a wooden handle. The bucket drifts further out to sea. The next day, he wakes up, yawns loudly, and says, "Oh, I'm in a bucket!" He swims out of the bucket sluggishly. Once he's fully awake, he swims at a normal pace into a deeper part of the ocean.

CHAPTER 3

THE SHIPWRECK

The little axolotl explores the sea during the day and looks for a new place to sleep. He swims slowly up to the ocean's surface to get air. As he inhales more air, he enjoys the smell of salt. Even though the axolotl is a freshwater species, he quickly adapts to the saltwater ocean.

The axolotl sees a lot of kelp waving in the ocean currents, seagrass, and an ocean ruin with stone walls that are crumbling. Eventually, he finds a shipwreck big enough to sleep in. He swims cautiously into its hull and then up to its deck. Suddenly, while he's sleeping on the top deck of his wooden ship, one of the unstable planks breaks and he drifts below the deck.

Several minutes later, a curious-looking person with netherite armor and a special water-breathing effect coming from his body walks through a large crack onto the old wooden hull. His netherite armor is well forged. He says, "Who's there? Oh, there's a little axolotl!"

The axolotl says sleepily, "Hello, I was just trying to get back to sleep in this old shipwreck."

The mysterious person asks, "Can I carry you in my bucket?"

"Why do you want me in your bucket?" the confused axolotl asks.

The person says, "I'm looking for treasure. I think you can help me find more treasure, and we can become friends. My name is Doug."

The axolotl replies with a yawn, "Sure, I'll go with you." He was happy he'd found his first friend!

Doug continues to look around the shipwreck and finds a chest that contains a treasure map. It's handmade and made of papyrus. There is also a trident enchanted with loyalty and impaling. The new weapon glows with power. He knows it's good luck. The map shows a path to an ocean monument that he knows will have treasure. Doug scoops the axolotl into the bucket and begins to swim to the ocean monument as the axolotl falls asleep.

CHAPTER 4

BATTLE OF THE MONUMENT

When Doug gets to the ocean monument, he releases the axolotl out of the bucket. The little axolotl opens his eyes sluggishly and quietly says, "Whoa, this is a big temple!"

Doug says, "It's not a temple; it's a monument."

The axolotl asks, "What are these creatures I see? They look like giant pufferfish!"

Doug replies, "The green pufferfish are called guardians, and the tan ones are called elder guardians.

The axolotl says, "I'm still going to call them pufferfish."

Doug replies, "Have it your way, but they're very dangerous." Doug knows the guardians are trouble, but he thinks he can still find the treasure if he gets some support.

Doug previously collected five axolotls from other caves but forgot to map each cave. However, he can release them into the ocean monument to help if they need to battle the guardians. The guardians and elder guardians then take notice of Doug from far away. Suddenly, one of the guardians looks at Doug with its giant beady eye and shoots a tractor beam at him. Doug cannot swim away from the tractor beam because it keeps following him. He's also taking massive damage. He can't handle any more damage. He begins to release the other axolotls because the guardians are determined to see his destruction.

Doug uses the trident he found in the shipwreck, throwing it at the guardians. The trident glows light purple and strikes the guardian. The other guardians are too scared to fight anymore and leave the monument as fast as they can, not worrying about

Doug taking their treasure because Doug is determined to see their destruction now. Doug quickly releases the rest of his axolotl companions to help fight more guardians that might come later.

Suddenly, Doug sees something at the top of the monument. It's an elder guardian. The elder guardian stares at him closely, soon realizing that Doug is not from the monument. It then starts releasing all of the blue spines out of its body. It rushes toward Doug at terrifying speed and inflicts mining fatigue on Doug's soul.

Doug says, "Without my mining abilities, I can't hide!"

Suddenly, all of the axolotls face the elder guardian still rushing toward Doug. The axolotls attack the elder guardian all at once. The elder guardian starts picking off the axolotls one by one. Luckily, none of them are hurt and are just playing dead.

Soon enough, all of the axolotls are back in

the fight and destroy the elder guardian. It drops prismarine shards.

Doug says, "Thank you axolotls. These can be used to make prismarine blocks to help my base." As Doug holds the prismarine shards, he notices they're very strong. On the sandy ocean floor, Doug sees something slightly glowing in the sand. As he picks it up, he notices it's a crystal. He finds more crystals on the sandy floor. He comes to think that the crystals have been hidden in the sand for millions of years. The crystals slightly glow, and Doug prizes them. Doug soon tries turning them carefully into a block, but his experiment fails. He thinks that using the prismarine shards and connecting them with the polished crystals could work. This time his experiment did not fail! As soon as he merges the two components, they create a block that is a light source. It works perfectly, and he prizes the glowing block.

The axolotl says, "We still have to find your

treasure. I see more guardians in the distance rushing toward you!"

They quickly swim into the monument before the guardians can catch them, but it's too late. The guardians start using the tractor beam on Doug and the axolotls again, but this time Doug has a plan! Even though he has mining fatigue, he can still fight back. He tells the axolotls his plan. He says, "Attack the guardians while they follow me." Doug leads the guardians away from the axolotls. Soon, enough of the axolotls listen to his plan and start attacking the guardians.

One of the six axolotls says, "At this rate, we can defeat all of them in minutes." Doug and the axolotls finally defeat them!

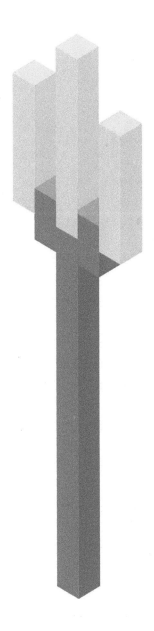

CHAPTER 5

ANCIENT TREASURES

With the guardians and elder guardians out of the way, Doug and the axolotls can use the treasure map to seek out the treasure room that Doug knows is hiding in the ocean monument. Suddenly, Doug sees a beady eye looking at him from one of the faraway rooms. It starts swimming at Doug very fast. Doug notices that it's another elder guardian and says, "Oh no, more trouble. I just lost my mining fatigue effect!" Suddenly, without command, all of the axolotls start to attack the elder guardian before it can attack them. It drops more prismarine shards and a sponge. Doug says, "I can use this to clear any water, or I can put it in my base as a trophy."

Doug can finally focus on getting the treasure again. The map shows where the treasure is hidden. The treasure is encased in dark prismarine blocks. Doug starts mining away the blocks and says, "I can also add these to my base." Behind the blocks are eight solid blocks of gold! The precious metal has no scratches or dents on it and is perfectly made. Doug wants to mine the solid blocks of gold, but first, he enchants his netherite pickaxe with fortune III. Doug quickly mines the gold and instead of getting eight blocks, gets fifteen!

They leave the ocean monument in horror. Doug thinks he's beaten all of the guardians, but he's wrong. Hundreds of guardians start swimming at them from every direction! Luckily, Doug doesn't have mining fatigue anymore. All of the guardians are in danger. He grabs his enchanting table and lays his netherite sword on the soft leather. The enchanting table does its work, and soon Doug's sword is glowing with power. He grips his sword as hard as he can, and it glows with fire. He slices one of the guardians, and it starts to burn fiercely. Even though the guardians are underwater, Doug enchants fire aspect III on his sword in such a way that anything will burn to a crisp. Doug also enchants his sword with the highest level of knockback. As he strikes a guardian lightly with his sword, it flies backward into a prismarine wall.

The coast seems to be clear. Doug hits every guardian lightly, and they all go away leaving lots of loot for him to pick up. He walks back into the ocean monument and discovers a hidden chest. As he opens the chest, he sees jewels of diamond, emerald, and lapis lazuli and precious metals of iron and gold! Doug scoops up all of the axolotls into their respective buckets. Doug quickly swims up to the surface and grabs onto his birch boat. He jumps on it and starts rowing to the nearest shore. As the boat docks onto the sandy beach, Doug steps out on the shore near his base. Suddenly, a small wave sweeps him backward. Luckily, Doug knows how to swim and swims back onto the sandy shore. For safety, he checks to see if he has all of his gold blocks. "One, two, three…fourteen and done," Doug sighed. I should have laid them all out on the sand for an easier way of counting.

CHAPTER 6

HIDDEN BASE

To bring the gold back to Doug's base, the axolotl and Doug go to the area where his base is. The axolotl says, "Why does this mountain look so familiar?"

Doug replies, "I don't know."

The axolotl says, "Where's the base?"

Doug replies, "Watch and learn!" Doug goes over to a normal tree.

The axolotl says, "There's nothing here!"

Doug finds a lever and pulls it. It opens up a tunnel.

The axolotl says, "Whoa, you know how to use redstone!

Doug replies, "Yes."

The axolotl says, "What are you going to do with the gold blocks?"

Doug replies, "I'm going to use them as stands for my trophies."

The confused axolotl says, "But there's no trophy room in your base."

Doug replies, "Watch and learn."

Doug pushes a stone button on a wall, and it opens up a secret quartz-walled room.

The axolotl yells, "Wow!"

Doug walks into the room and puts down the gold blocks. He lays soft velvet fabric on the gold and slowly places a prismarine shard on the fabric on the blocks with care. Then he encloses the blocks with glass panes.

The axolotl says, "No one can steal them now."

Doug replies, "Do you like my trophy room?"

The axolotl yells loudly, "This is amazing!"

They leave the trophy room, and Doug pushes the button to close the room.

CHAPTER 7

THE AQUARIUM

The axolotl says, "I really need somewhere to stay. It's too tight in this bucket."

Doug replies, "OK, I'll make you an aquarium."

Several minutes later, Doug starts to make the aquarium. He makes it big enough to fit six axolotls. He adds a sand bottom for the axolotls to sleep on. He has some aquatic plants, and he arranges them on the aquarium's sand floor. He also adds some coral to brighten the aquarium. Doug slowly releases the axolotl into his new aquarium. The axolotl's leg is the first thing to touch the water.

"It's just right," says the axolotl. As he enters the water, he knows that it's freshwater. The axolotl is very pleased to be in his new aquarium and out of his tight bucket.

Doug puts the bucket into one of his treasure chests and says, "OK, I may need this later to transport you somewhere else." He closes the chest and sighs.

The axolotl says, "Even though I'm in this wonderful aquarium, I still want to go home to my lush caves."

"I'll find your home again," Doug promises.

The axolotl suddenly yawns. He swims down to the bottom of the aquarium and lays on the sand. Doug walks over to his chest again. He puts the rest of the building materials in his chest. He slowly walks to his bedroom. He lays on his bed and falls asleep.

CHAPTER 8

FINDING THE LUSH CAVES

The next morning, the axolotl wakes up and opens his eyes slowly. He's tangled in the aquatic plants. He starts to swim, but it's no use. He calls Doug from under the water to help him. Doug rushes to the front of the aquarium and says, "Oh, no!" Doug puts his hands into the aquarium and untangles the plants, freeing the axolotl.

Doug gives the axolotl his usual breakfast of mollusks and sits on his chair facing the axolotl. Doug says, "Let's think of some ideas to get to your lush caves."

They have lots of good ideas. Doug's first idea is to use their memories to remember where the axolotl came from, but the axolotl doesn't remember, except that he came out of a passageway and that the mountain outside the base looks familiar.

Doug's second idea is to make a telescope. The axolotl says, "We should be able to see a passageway with a telescope."

CHAPTER 9

MAKING A TELESCOPE

"The first step to make a telescope is to get some crystal shards," Doug says. "No problem," the axolotl replies, "We only need one crystal shard."

Doug has a room in his base that leads to a huge geode that is full of crystals. Doug's theory is that billions of years ago, the cave was filled with saltwater and no crystals. But with heat and pressure, the saltwater dried out and crystals were left.

"Do you like my theory?" Doug asks.

"Yes, your theory is very interesting," the axolotl replies.

Doug puts the axolotl back in the bucket, and they head out to the huge geode. Doug takes off one of the crystal shards and says, "This will do!"

"Yes, it's the right size," says the axolotl.

Doug says, "Wait! We can't just put an uncut crystal into a telescope; we must polish it."

The axolotl replies, "OK, I guess that makes sense."

Doug walks over to his stonecutter. He focuses on cutting the right angles on the crystal shard. "And... Done!" Doug yells. Doug holds the polished crystal up to the light and says, "Perfect!"

"The second ingredient we need is copper ore," the axolotl says.

"I don't have any on hand right now," Doug sighs. "Maybe we can find some in my new mineshaft."

Doug walks to the mineshaft and slowly mines away the stone and gravel. Doug finds some copper ore. He has the idea of making a lightning rod because his region in the world has lots of lightning strikes. He continues to mine the copper vein and suddenly falls through the wall and is shocked to find himself in a lush cave!

CHAPTER 10

RETURN OF THE LUSH CAVES

Doug says to the axolotl, "Oh, my gosh! You've got to see this!" He turns the axolotl's bucket around so that he can see what he's talking about.

The axolotl replies, "Wow! Those are the lush caves that I came from!"

Doug smiles and says, "Now that we have found your home, I think I should name you. I think your name should be 'Geode' because your skin has the exact color as the geode where I get my crystals."

"Thank you, I love that name," says the axolotl.

Doug joins the lush caves to his base by breaking a hole in the wall big enough for him to pass through so that they're connected. Doug brings the five other axolotl buckets to the lush caves so that Geode will have some new friends to play with. The five axolotls are tinted yellow and look different from Geode.

They also recognize the lush caves as being their old home before they left. Geode also now remembers that they were his friends before they had to leave the lush caves because there was a drought and the pond was divided into two parts, separated by sand they couldn't cross. Geode was stuck alone on the other side and never saw them again until now. Geode welcomes them home. They're all reunited!

Geode starts swimming in his pond. He says, "Just as I remember it." He brushes up against one of the walls in his excitement, which triggers a chain reaction. Suddenly, gravel on the bottom of the pond falls. Luckily, Geode is safe. When the gravel finally stops falling, a gaping hole is left. Geode gasps, "Where does this lead?"

Doug replies, "I guess we're going to find out!"

"But we have no building materials; we won't be able to get down there," says Geode.

"Wait a moment, please. I'll be right back," replies Doug.

Doug walks back into his room. He opens a chest and grabs out some building materials. The materials are: white stained glass and diorite stairs. The beautiful diorite is an excellent choice of stone, prized for its white coloration. He walks back to the lush caves where Geode lives.

Geode says, "What are we going to do?"

Doug replies, "I'm going to build a stairway down into the cave below your lush caves."

He starts building the stairway and surrounds the stairway with the white stained glass to keep out the freshwater ponds and to keep the stairs dry.

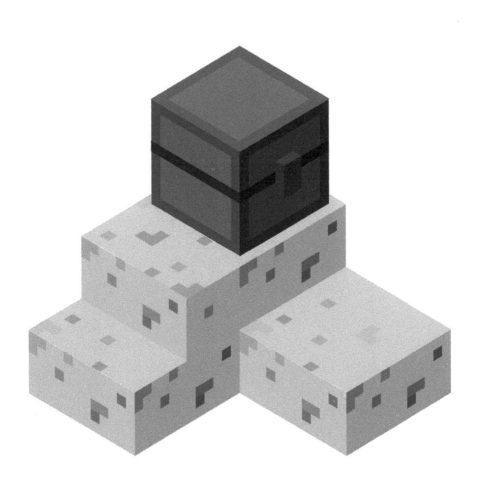

CHAPTER 11
THE DEEP DARK

D oug walks down the stairs he created, holding Geode's transporting bucket. Once Doug finally gets to the bottom of the stairway, he says, "I can barely see anything in these caves."

Geode replies, "Look over there! I see light!"

"Good point," Doug says. Doug walks toward the light slowly. He suddenly gasps, "This is a whole building!"

Geode says, "It's not really like a building; it's more like a cabin that was built a long time ago. But by whom?"

Doug walks into the abandoned building and yells, "Just what I've been looking for: candles!"

Suddenly, before Doug can start mining the mysterious candles, they start dimming and brightening. The candle wax seems to melt more slowly than usual.

Geode asks, "What's happening?"

Doug replies, "I just figured out what type of cave this is. It's really rare, and it's called the 'deep dark cave.'" Unexpectedly, a loud groan echoes through the cavern.

Geode whispers, "What's that?"

Doug tells him it's a warden. Doug says, "It's blind, so it can't see us, right?"

Geode replies, "I don't know."

Suddenly, the warden walks close to them.

Doug whispers to Geode, "It can't see us, so we're safe."

Suddenly, vibrations from Doug's mouth go right to the warden's horns. The horns glow blue for a second and then fade. The warden turns its head and starts running directly toward Doug. Doug yells, "I totally forgot that wardens can hear all your vibrations. I have a plan for this."

Doug has a snowball in his inventory and throws it very far away outside the cabin. The snowball lands with few sounds and disintegrates except for a couple of pieces of snow on the stone floor. The warden detects the snowball's vibration and quickly darts to where the snowball lands.

Doug whispers, "I think we're safe." Suddenly, the warden starts to run at Doug again. Doug pulls out his netherite sword enchanted with all the enchantments he knows. He slashes at the warden. Usually, he can destroy anything he slashes on the first try, but his strategy does not work this time. Doug gets hit by the warden and falls on the ground with weakness, but he survives the blow, barely. Doug starts slashing at the warden multiple times. Doug grabs one of his other snowballs and throws it in an opposite direction. As usual, the warden follows the vibrations.

Doug slowly follows the warden. Doug cannot handle slashing the warden anymore, so he drinks a potion with an effect of strength II. He stabs the warden with his sword as hard as he can, and the warden falls to the ground, dropping nothing!

Doug says, "No fair...Anyway, I should start mining those candles." He walks over to the candles. Instead of mining the candles, he picks up each candle individually. They do not burn his hands and merely drip candle wax on them. He blows out the candles' flames and puts them in his inventory. The walls and floors of this cave look pretty cool. "Because this cave is called a deep dark cave, I'm going to call this stone 'darkstone.'"

Suddenly, another groan is heard in the cave, but it has a lighter tone to it. Doug wonders if it's a baby warden. He looks around every corner in the deep cave but sees nothing. He sits down on the floor wondering where the sound is coming from. When Doug realizes that the vibrations are going into the ground, he stands up and walks toward where the vibrations are being received. Suddenly, he trips and falls onto the cave floor.

The ground glows cyan blue for a second and dims. Doug says, "This patch of ground seems to be related to the warden." He whispers to himself, "Now how am I going to mine this?" He puts his finger onto the patch of ground. "It seems to be a relative of dirt. So, I guess I'll use a hoe to mine it," he says. He pulls out his netherite hoe from one of his pockets and starts tilling the mysterious patch of the substance. The new type of soil starts crumbling under the pressure of the hoe. Doug is able to find a few large pieces of the new soil to put in his inventory. The same type of soil in the area detects the vibrations of the crumbling soil.

Doug asks Geode, "What would you call this new type of soil?"

Geode answers, "Because it looks like it's sulking, I'm going to call it a 'sculk,' and the second word, because it can detect vibrations, is 'sensor.' So, I'll call this new type of soil a 'sculk sensor.'"

Doug walks back up to the stairs and is in the lush caves again. He walks into his laboratory and tests the soil he collected from the deep dark. Doug whispers, "Every time it detects a vibration, it can power redstone." Then he yells, "I can use this for a better entrance to my base!" Doug tells Geode about his ideas for his new base entrance.

"I love it!" Geode says enthusiastically.

Doug grabs most of the redstone, repeaters, pistons, sticky pistons, and comparators.

CHAPTER 12

THE DRIPSTONE CAVES

Several minutes later, Doug starts recreating his base entrance so that he can enter the base without activating the base opener button.

"You're doing great so far," Geode says.

Doug grabs his pickaxe and starts mining some of the wall so he can fill it in with redstone wiring. He reaches into his pocket and grabs the sculk sensor.

Doug whispers, "Now if I were to connect this redstone wiring to the sculk sensor, it should be able to send powerful enough signals to power the door to open." He connects the wire. His voice has vibrations, and he opens the door with his mouth vibrations!

Doug whispers again, "I don't want my voice to activate the door because then anyone can enter. I know—I'll use a comparator to make movement create vibrations to open the door, not sounds."

Geode says, "Good thinking."

Doug quickly grabs some comparators and wires them so sounds will not make vibrations. Geode tells Doug that anyone can still enter because they can just walk up to the door, and it'll open.

Doug replies, "Good point. I'm going to keep wiring the door so that it'll only detect my own vibrations." After five minutes, Doug finishes wiring his door to fit his needs.

Geode says, "Perfect!"

Doug adds, "Wait, I just noticed something. If I trigger the vibrations while I'm inside my base, and there is a monster outside my base...that means that the monster can come in while the door is open. If I keep wiring it, I'll have to redo the whole door. But, I can make potions to help myself whenever a monster comes in."

Geode says, "But I looked at your cauldron lately, and every time you need more water for potions, you have to walk all the way to the ocean to get it."

Doug replies, "I see what you're saying, but we need a way to get water without going all the way to the ocean. Hmm, I don't know how we're going to do it yet. We'll try to find a source in my base. Wait! I know where we can get water—your lush caves!"

Geode says, "But my lush caves do not regenerate their water. If you keep taking water from my lush caves, there will be no more water left."

Doug replies, "Good point. Where else can we find water?"

Geode says, "I don't know."

Doug replies, "Well, you can go back into your lush caves. I'll be mining."

Doug took Geode to the lush caves. He walks to his new mine to mine for ores, but as soon as he starts mining, he falls through a small gap in his new mine. He starts falling ten feet downward and hits his body on a stalagmite. Luckily, he's OK, but very badly injured!

When he's able to stand up straight again, he looks upward and has no building materials, and so he can't go back up into the start of his mine. He soon realizes that he has no help since Geode is in his own lush caves. Doug is practically trapped in this new cave. Doug looks around the area for new building materials. He can see no building materials except stone. He also notices giant stalagmites and stalactites forming from the ground and from the ceiling. Sometimes the stalagmites and stalactites connect with each other, forming a column.

He looks upward onto the top of the cave and soon realizes that some stalactites are dripping water. Luckily, he has a pickaxe to mine the stalactites, stalagmites, and the stone. As he stocks up on stone and a few pieces of stalactites, he's ready to build right back up to his mine. Doug thinks to himself, *This time the stone is not polished, and because it's natural, I like the look of it.*

Once he finishes the stairway to his mine, he quickly walks to his laboratory to test a stalactite. He sees that water is dripping from the stalactite whenever he puts water on top of the block the stalactite is on. This also works with lava. He theorizes to himself, *When I put water above the block the stalactite is hanging on, some of the water goes into the core of the stalactite, forcing some of the water to drip out.* Doug says, "This will fit all my needs for potion making." He then shows Geode the new cave he discovered.

Geode exclaims, "This is amazing!"

Doug replies, "Right, these stalactites are the key to getting water."

Geode adds, "Good, I guess we could expand my lush caves."

Doug replies, "Good idea!"

Soon the lush caves are finished, and more axolotls are added to the caves. One day, Doug walks up to Geode and says, "I have a new friend for you."

Geode smiles with excitement. Doug is holding a similar bucket to Geode's, but it's made of steel rather than iron. Doug releases the axolotl into the caves.

Geode says, "How did you find this breed of axolotl? It's super rare."

Doug replies, "Easy, I found two of the same breed of axolotls and bred them and created this small axolotl about your size."

Geode says, "Thank you. Are you going to name him?"

Doug replies, "I'll name him 'Blurple.'"

Geode says, "That's an excellent name." Blurple was very happy to be with Geode, and they're best friends!

AXOLOTL

FACT FILE

- This special type of salamander lives only in the canals and rivers in regions of Mexico like Lake Xochimilco.

- Axolotls can even regrow limbs. If one of an axolotl's limbs is removed, it'll regrow the limb in a short amount of time, specifically, in 40 to 50 days.

- You may have recognized what an axolotl looks like. Its body is milky pink, and its gills are slightly darker, but wild axolotls are usually a shade of brown colored to match the mud of the rivers in Mexico. The axolotl has many variants of colors including golden, albino, pink, and a wild variant.

- Axolotls often seem to have emotions on their faces. Mostly you can see his or her little smiley face smiling back at you.

- Axolotls may seem cute, but they're actually predators. They eat small fish, tadpoles, other salamanders, and small crustaceans.

- Also, you may notice and wonder where the gills on the axolotls' heads are. Strangely, the gills of the axolotl are the feathery limbs coming from the sides of their heads.

- The main reason axolotls are endangered is that big fish that live in the same rivers and ponds that axolotls thrive in eat the axolotls' small eggs. There are other reasons too, such as pollution and the size of their home decreasing from human population expansion.

- The axolotl was chosen as the first official national emoji for Mexico City and is also the first city to launch an official emoji.

Farewell

See you in our next adventure in book 2, *The Axolotl: Iceberg Adventures in Minecraft*

THE **AXOLOTL** ICEBERG ADVENTURES IN MINECRAFT

HAYDEN COLES

NOT AN OFFICIAL MINECRAFT PRODUCT NOT APPROVED BY OR ASSOCIATED WITH MOJANG

Doug and Geode

CPSIA information can be obtained
at www.ICGtesting.com
Printed in the USA
LVHW052253101121
702881LV00011B/291

25. S. Gifford, *PETA's Letter to Safeway Explaining That the Decision to Treat Animals with Basic Decency Is Up to Safeway*, 2001, http://www.goveg.com/shameway_let9-14.asp (accessed March 15, 2007).

26. H. Mayer, *Animal Welfare Verification in Canada*, Canadian Council of Grocery Distributors, 2002, http://www.facs.sk.ca/pdf/other/animal_welfare_verification_Canada.pdf (accessed March 15, 2007).

27. Canadian Federation of Humane Societies, "McDonald's and Burger King Leading the Way," 2002, http://cfhs.ca/info/mcdonald%E2_s_and_burger_king_leading_the_way/ (accessed March 15, 2007).

28. C. Bylin, R. Misra, M. Murch, and W. Rigterink, *Sustainable Agriculture: An On-Farm Assessment Tool* (Ann Arbor, MI: University of Michigan, 2004).

29. H. Kawachi, "Micronutrients Affecting Adipogenesis in Beef Cattle," *Animal Science Journal* 77 (2006): 463–471.

30. J. Longworth, *Beef in Japan* (Brisbane: University of Queensland Press, 1983).

31. J. Reynolds, *The Great Paternalist* (London: Maurice Temple Smith, 1983). The quote is on page 89.

32. R. Balgarnie, *Sir Titus Salt, Baronet* (Settle, Yorkshire: Brenton Publishing, 1877). The quote is on page 135.

33. Ibid., 38.

EPILOGUE

1. Food and Agriculture Organization of the United Nations, *State of Food Insecurity in the World 2006* (Rome: FAO, 2006).

35. H. Brayer, "The Influence of British Capital on the Western Range-Cattle Industry," *Journal of Economic History* 9 (1949): 85–98.

36. D. Galenson, "The End of the Chisholm Trail," *Journal of Economic History* 34 (1974): 350–364.

37. E. Dale, "The Cow Country in Transition," *Mississippi Valley Historical Review* 24 (1937): 3–20. The quote is on pages 7 and 8.

38. W. Webb, *The Great Plains* (Waltham, MA: Ginn and Company, 1931).

39. R. Dykstra, *The Cattle Towns* (Lincoln: University of Nebraska Press, 1968).

40. C. Hutson, "Texas Fever in Kansas, 1866–1930," *Agricultural History* 68 (1994): 74–104. The quote is on page 81.

41. Hutson, "Texas Fever in Kansas, 1866–1930," 80.

42. M. Welch, "The Spanish Fever: How They Treat Texas Cattle on the Border," *Prairie Farmer* 39 (1868), 98.

43. Hutson, "Texas Fever in Kansas."

44. R. Dennen, "Cattle Trailing in the Nineteenth Century," *Journal of Economic History* 35 (1975): 458–460.

45. Devil's Rope Museum, "A Brief History of Barbed Wire," Devil's Rope Museum, McLean Texas, 2007, http://www.barbwiremuseum.com/index.htm (accessed August 14, 2007).

46. J. McFadden, "Monopoly in Barbed Wire: The Formation of the American Steel and Wire Company," *The Business History Review* 52 (1978): 465–489.

47. Texas Beef Council, Beef Recipes, 2007, http://www.txbeef.org/recipe.php3?944688139 (accessed July 16, 2007).

48. A. Davidson, *Oxford Companion to Food* (Oxford: Oxford University Press, 1999).

49. J. Williams, *Wagonwheel Kitchens: Food on the Oregon Trail* (Lawrence: University of Kansas Press, 1993).

50. M. Marchello and J. Garden-Robinson, "Jerky Making: Then and Now, *North Dakota State University's College of Agriculture, Food Systems and Natural Resources*, 1999, http://www.ag.ndsu.edu/pubs/yf/foods/fn580w.htm (accessed August 14, 2007).

51. The Chicago Historical Society's Homepage, *The Birth of the Chicago Union Stock Yards*, 2001, http://www.chicagohs.org/history/stockyard/stock1.html (accessed August 31, 2007).

52. U. Sinclair, *The Jungle* (New York: Penguin, 1985). The quote is on page 98.

53. Ibid., 120.

54. For a discussion on the origins of this poem, see *Cowboy Poetry*, 2007, http://www.cowboypoetry.com/whoknows4.htm#Longhorn (accessed July 16, 2007).

CHAPTER 6

1. Three Dales Quality Local Meat Web Page, http://www.threedales.co.uk/index.php (accessed May 31, 2007).

2. Meat Info, online Meat Trades Journal, 2007, http://www.meatinfo.co.uk/ (accessed, March 15, 2007).

3. Osborn Samuel Gallery, *Biography of Peter Kinley*, 2007, http://osbornesamuel.com/pages/biography/41088.html (accessed March 15, 2007).

4. J. Clay, *World Agriculture and the Environment* (Washington, DC: Island Press, 2004).

5. National Agricultural Statistics Service, "All Cattle & Beef Cows: Number of Operations by Year, US," http://www.nass.usda.gov/Charts_and_Maps/Cattle/acbc_ops.asp (accessed March 16, 2007).

6. For a review of popular works on this subject, please see J. Rifkin, *Beyond Beef* (New York: Plume, 1993); A. Kimbrell, ed., *The Fatal Harvest Reader: The Tragedy of Industrial Agriculture* (Washington, DC: Island Press, 2002); E. Schlosser, *Fast Food Nation* (London: Allen Lane, 2001).

7. Metropolitan Museum of Art, Details on John Curry, Collection Highlights, http://www.metmuseum.org/Works_of_Art/viewOne.asp?dep=21&viewmode=0&item=42.154 (accessed March 16, 2007).

8. U.S. Department of Agriculture, "Changes in Size and Location of U.S. Dairy Farms," in *Profits, Costs, and the Changing Structure of Dairy Farming* / ERR-47 Economic Research Service, USDA, 2006.

9. D. Jackson-Smith and B. Barham, "Dynamics of Dairy Industry Restructuring in Wisconsin," in *Dairy Industry Restructuring: Research in Rural Sociology and Development*, vol. 8, eds. H. Schwarzweller and A. Davidson (Amsterdam: JAI, 2000). Please see page 115.

10. R. Knutson and R. Loyns, "Understanding Canadian/United States Dairy Disputes," in *Proceedings of the Second Annual Canada/U.S. Agricultural*

and Food Policy Systems Information Workshop, eds. R. Knutson and R. Loyns (Guelph, Canada: University of Guelph, 1996).

11. W. Butler and C. Wolf, "California Dairy Production: Unique Policies and Natural Advantages," in *Dairy Industry Restructuring: Research in Rural Sociology and Development*, vol. 8, eds. H. Schwarzweller and A. Davidson (Amsterdam: JAI, 2000).

12. Food and Agriculture Association, *Livestock's Long Shadow* (Rome: United Nations, 2006).

13. A. Hovey, "Nebraska Hog, Cattle Farmers Take Losses as Grain Prices Soar," *Lincoln Journal Star*, May 2, 2008, http://www.siouxcityjournal.com/articles/2008/04/13/news/latest_news/doc4802161024de8996013082.txt (accessed May 2, 2008).

14. J. Steinbeck, *The Grapes of Wrath* (New York: Penguin, 2002).

15. J. Lawrence, "Impact of Higher Corn Prices on Feed Costs," *Iowa Farm Outlook*, October 1–2, 2006.

16. W. E. Riebsame, S. A. Changnon, and T. R. Karl. *Drought and Natural Resource Management in the United States* (Boulder, CO: Westview Press, 1991).

17. K. R. Laird, S. C. Fritz, K. A. Maasch, and B. F. Cumming, "Greater Drought Intensity and Frequency Before A.D. 1200 in the Northern Great Plains, U.S.A," *Nature* 384 (1996): 552–554.

18. N. Rosenberg, D. Epstein, D. Wang, L. Vail, R. Srinivasan, and J. Arnold, "Possible Impacts of Global Warming on the Hydrology of the Ogallala Aquifer Region," *Climatic Change* 42 (1999): 677–692.

19. Texas Water Development Board, *Surveys of Irrigation in Texas 1958, 1964, 1969, 1974, 1979, 1984, 1989, and 1994*. Report no. 347. (Austin: Texas Water Development Board, 1996).

20. B. Terrell, P. N. Johnson, and E. Segarra, "Ogallala Aquifer Depletion: Economic Impact on the Texas High Plains," *Water Policy* (2002), 4, 33–46.

21. E. Lambin, B. Turner, H. Geist, S. Agbola, A. Angelsen, J. Bruce, O. Coomes, et al., "The Causes of Land-Use and Land-Cover Change: Moving Beyond the Myths," *Global Environmental Change* 11 (2001): 261–269.

22. Food and Agriculture Association, *Livestock's Long Shadow*.

23. Interview with Lauren Gwin, December 31, 2007.

24. Mcspotlight, *The Mclibel Story*, 2007, http://www.mcspotlight.org (accessed March 15, 2007).

• INDEX •

dairy industry
    large-scale farms, 153, 184
    modern-day, xvii, 153, 179–82,
        183–84, 201–4
    small-scale farms, 150–53, 183–84
    sustainable practices, 201–4
dairy products. *See* cheese; cow's
    milk
Dale valleys, 149–52
Delamere cattle, 40
Dick o' the Cow, 96–97
disease. *See also* rinderpest
    bovine babesiosis, 155
    bovine pleuropneumonia, 134
    foot-and-mouth, 148, 178
    "foul vapors" theory, 144
    germ theory, 144–45, 148, 161
    government controls against, 148
    isolated plagues, 141
    mad cow, 148, 178
    quarantine measures, 145–46
    Rift Valley fever, 134
    Texas fever, 155, 161–62
    vaccinations against, 134–35
Dishley longhorns, 119–20, 121
domestication, animal, 21–28
domestication, plant, 22–23
The Domestication of Europe (Hod-
    der), 52
Donley-Reid, Linda, 51–52
Donn Cuailnge, 19, 78
drought, 23–24, 185–89
"dual-purpose" cattle, 194–95
Dumuzi the shepherd, 28
dung, 26, 117, 182, 191
Dust Bowl, 186, 187
Dutch Holstein, 153

E
E. coli, 152, 178
Egyptian bull worship, 64–66

Egyptian cheese makers, 85
Eighty Years War, 105–6
El (Bull El), 69–70
El Fundi, 34
Eliot, T. S., 185
Elizabeth I, Queen of England, 106
Emmenthal cheese, 91
Epic of Gilgamesh (Sumerian leg-
    end), 56–57
Europa, 58
Exodus, Book of, 68–71
Ezekiel, Book of, 48

F
farmers, Anatolian, 22–23
farmers, Neolithic, 23, 24, 26–28,
    51, 82
fast food restaurants, 199–200
feedlots, 181–82, 186–87, 196–97
fences, barbed-wire, 162
Ferdinand III, King of Castille, 128
Fertile Crescent, 26
fertility cult, Neolithic, 50
fertility goddesses, 63
flank cuts, 16
flatulence, 12
Fontina Val D'Aosta cheese, 91
Food and Agriculture Organization
    of the United Nations, 184,
    194
foot-and-mouth disease, 148, 178
The Forme of Cury, 93–94
"foul vapors" theory, 144
Fraech, 79–80
Frazer, James, 61–63

G
Gainsborough, Thomas, 111–13, 121
Gamgee, John, 143, 144, 145, 148,
    161
gauchos, 125–26